Silly People Rhymes

Cover illustration by JON GOODELL

Illustrations by
KRISTA BRAUCKMANN-TOWNS
JANE CHAMBLESS WRIGHT
DREW-BROOK-CORMACK ASSOCIATES
KATE STURMAN GORMAN
JUDITH DUFOUR LOVE
BEN MAHAN
ANASTASIA MITCHELL
ANITA NELSON
ROSARIO VALDERRAMA

Louis Weber, C.E.O.
Publications International, Ltd.
7373 North Cicero Avenue
Lincolnwood, Illinois 60646

Permission is never granted for commercial purposes.

Manufactured in U.S.A.

8 7 6 5 4 3 2 1

ISBN: 0-7853-1650-7

PUBLICATIONS INTERNATIONAL, LTD.

Rainbow Books is a trademark of Publications International, Ltd.

Handy Pandy

Handy Pandy, Jack-a-dandy,
Loves plum cake and sugar candy.

He bought some at a grocer's shop,
And out he came, hop, hop, hop.

Solomon Grundy

Solomon Grundy,
  Born on Monday,
Christened on Tuesday,
  Married on Wednesday,
Took ill on Thursday,
  Worse on Friday,
Died on Saturday,
  Buried on Sunday.
This is the end of Solomon Grundy.

The House That Jack Built

This is the farmer sowing his corn,
   That kept the rooster that crowed in the morn,
That waked the priest all shaven and shorn,
   That married the man all tattered and torn,
That kissed the maiden all forlorn,
   That milked the cow with the crumpled horn,
That tossed the dog,
   That worried the cat,
That killed the rat,
   That ate the malt,
That lay in the house that Jack built.

The Old Woman

The old woman stands at the tub, tub, tub,
   The dirty clothes to rub, rub, rub;
But when they are clean and fit to be seen,
   She'll dress like a lady and dance on the green.

Peter White

Peter White will ne'er go right,
    And would you know the reason why?
He follows his nose wherever he goes,
    And all that stands awry.

The Piper's Son

Tom, Tom, the piper's son,
  Stole a pig and away he run!
The pig thought it was quite a treat
  To be carried down the street.

Nothing-at-All

There was an old woman called Nothing-at-all,
  Who lived in a dwelling exceedingly small;
A man stretched his mouth to the utmost extent,
  And down in one gulp house and old woman went.

Rub-a-Dub-Dub

Rub-a-dub-dub,
   Three men in a tub,
And how do you think they got there?
   The butcher, the baker,
The candlestick maker,
   They all jumped out of a rotten potato,
'Twas enough to make a man stare.

Mary, Mary

Mary, Mary, quite contrary,
　How does your garden grow?
With silver bells and cockleshells,
　And pretty maids all in a row.

Lucy Locket

Lucy Locket lost her pocket,
Kitty Fisher found it;
Not a penny was there in it,
Only ribbon round it.

Gregory Griggs

Gregory Griggs, Gregory Griggs,
   Had twenty-seven different wigs.
He wore them up, he wore them down,
   To please the people of the town.
He wore them east, he wore them west,
   And never could tell which one he liked best.

The Old Woman
Under the Hill

There was an old woman
    Lived under a hill;
And if she's not gone,
    She lives there still.